Note to Readers

The title *The Frog in the Well* is a Chinese idiom or chéng yǔ. Chinese idioms are frequently used in Chinese language. They usually consist of four characters. Each idiom has a story based on folklore, myth, or a historical fact, and demonstrates a moral teaching.

This is a Chinese-English bilingual book with both traditional and simplified Chinese characters, along with its Zhu Yin Fu Hao and Pinyin. Both systems are phonetic notations for learning to read, write, and speak Mandarin. For more in-depth understanding, please refer to other books.

A Short Explanation of Pinyin

Pinyin is a phonetic notation that uses the Roman alphabet to represent sounds in Mandarin Chinese. Some alphabets do not correspond to an exact sound in English. For example, the letter "c" followed by a vowel is pronounced "ts". The list below will help readers pronounce the characters using Pinyin.

Letter followed by a vowel	Pronounced as
c	ts
q	ch
x	sh
z	dz
zh	j

jǐng　dǐ　zhī　wā ←——→ Pinyin

井ㄐㄥˇ 底ㄉㄧˇ 之ㄓ 蛙ㄨㄚ

Zhu Yin Fu Hao

Irene Y. Tsai
In loving memory of my mother, Fu-Jung

Pattie Caprio
To my parents, Lillian and Michael Caprio

CE Bilingual Books LLC
P.O. Box 31848
Philadelphia, PA 19104-1848
www.cebilingualbooks.com

THE FROG IN THE WELL

jǐng   dǐ   zhī   wā

Retold by Irene Y. Tsai
Chinese translation by *Joyce Lin*
Illustrations by *Pattie Caprio*

Publisher's Cataloging-in-Publication Data
Tsai, Irene, Y.
The frog in the well = Jing di zhi wa /written by Irene Y. Tsai,
Illustrated by Pattie Caprio
p. cm.

Summary: "The Frog in the Well" is a Chinese idiom to describe a
narrow-minded person. The frog hops happily in the well until the
turtle tells him about the world outside the well.

ISBN-13 978-0-9801305-1-5
ISBN-10 0-9801305-1-4

[1. Frogs - Fiction. 2. Fables - Chinese. 3. Picture books for children.
4. Chinese language materials - Bilingual. 5. Juvenile literature.
6. Language: Parallel texts in traditional Chinese script and English.]
I. Pattie Caprio, ill. II. Title.

J398.2095 T782J
j495.1/Tsai
JPic T7825f

Library of Congress Control Number 2008903491

Printed in Taiwan

THE FROG IN THE WELL

jǐng dǐ zhī wā
井底之蛙

中英對照
Chinese - English Bilingual Book

3

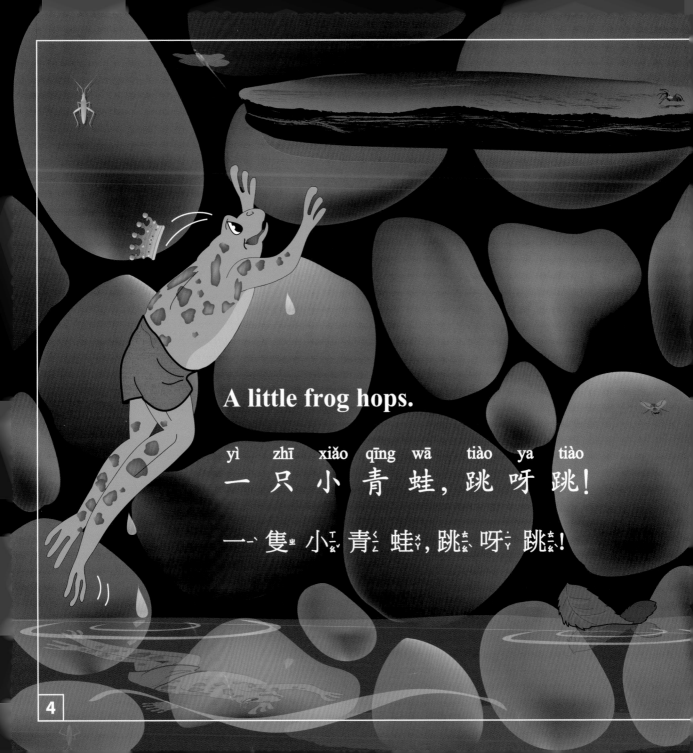

A little frog hops.

yì   zhī   xiǎo   qīng   wā   tiào   ya   tiào
一 只 小 青 蛙，跳 呀 跳!

一 隻 小 青 蛙，跳 呀 跳!

4

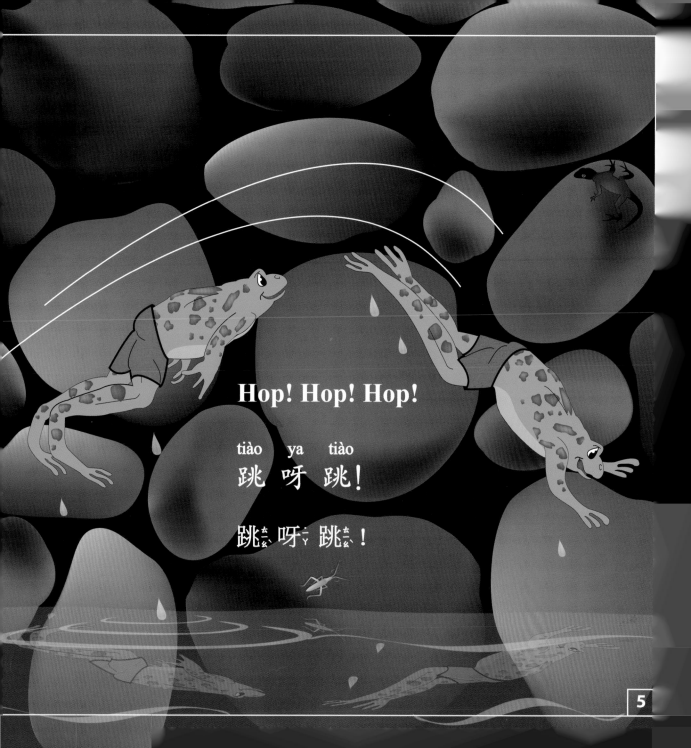

Hop! Hop! Hop!

tiào　　ya　　tiào
跳　呀　跳！

跳ㄊㄧㄠˋ呀ㄧㄚ跳ㄊㄧㄠˋ！

A well with shallow water.

yì kǒu shuǐ hěn qiǎn de jǐng
一 口 水 很 浅 的 井。
一ˋ 口ˇ 水ˇ 很ˇ 淺ˇ 的˙ 井ˇ。

The frog hops in the well.

qīng wā zài jǐng lǐ tiào ya tiào
青 蛙 在 井 里 跳 呀 跳。

青ㄑㄧㄥ 蛙ㄨㄚ 在ㄗㄞ 井ㄐㄧㄥ 裏ㄌㄧ 跳ㄊㄧㄠ 呀ㄧㄚ 跳ㄊㄧㄠ。

Splash! Splash! Splash!

pū tōng pū tōng pū tōng shuǐ huā pō chū lái
扑 通， 扑 通， 扑 通， 水 花 泼 出 来！

撲ㄨ 通ㄥ， 撲ㄨ 通ㄥ， 撲ㄨ 通ㄥ， 水ㄨ 花ㄚ 潑ㄨ 出ㄨ 來ㄞ！

The frog plunges into the water.

qīng wā pū tōng tiào xià shuǐ

青　蛙　扑　通　跳　下　水。

青 蛙 撲 通 跳 下 水 。

The frog is happy in the well.
"I know everything in the well.
I am the smartest frog in the world," the frog shouts.

qīng wā zài jǐng lǐ hěn kuài lè
青 蛙 在 井 里 很 快 乐。

zài jǐng lǐ wǒ jī hū shén me dōu zhī dào
"在 井 里，我 几 乎 什 么 都 知 道。

wǒ shì shì jiè shàng zuì cōng míng de qīng wā
我 是 世 界 上 最 聪 明 的 青 蛙。"

qīng wā dà shēng chàng
青 蛙 大 声 唱。

青蛙 在井 裏 很 快樂。

『在井 裏，我 幾乎 什麼 都 知 道。

我是 世 界上 最聰明 的 青 蛙。』

青蛙 大聲 唱。

When he is hungry,
he sticks his long tongue out
and rolls in a tiny fly.

dāng tā dù zi è le
当 他 肚 子 饿 了，
zhǐ yào shēn cháng shé tou
只 要 伸 长 舌 头，
jiù kě yǐ juǎn dào xiǎo cāng ying
就 可 以 卷 到 小 苍 蝇。

當他肚子餓了，
只要伸長舌頭，
就可以捲到小蒼蠅。

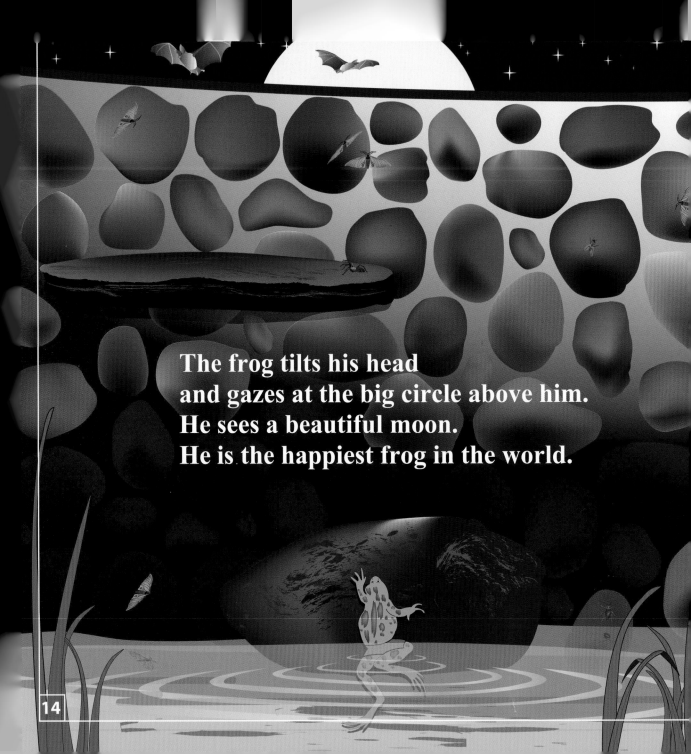

The frog tilts his head
and gazes at the big circle above him.
He sees a beautiful moon.
He is the happiest frog in the world.

青蛙抬起头来，
望着井口。
他看见一轮美丽的月亮。
他是世界上最快乐的青蛙了。

青蛙抬起頭來，
望著井口。
他看見一輪美麗的月亮。
他是世界上最快樂的青蛙了。

15

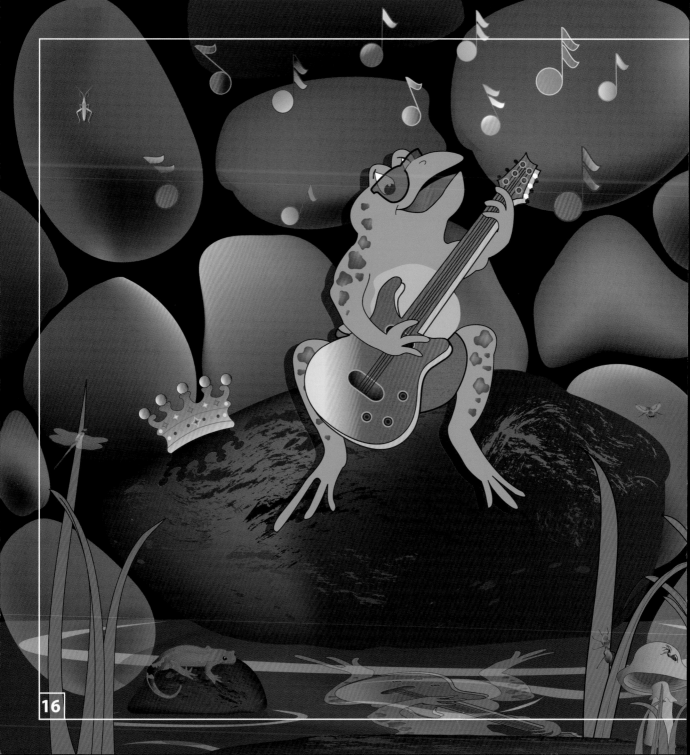

He sings a song as the clouds pass by.

dāng yì duǒ duo bái yún piāo guò
当 一 朵 朵 白 云 飘 过,
tā jiù chàng qǐ gē lái
他 就 唱 起 歌 来。

當ㄉㄤ 一ㄧˋ 朵ㄉㄨㄛˇ 朵ㄉㄨㄛˊ 白ㄅㄞˊ 雲ㄩㄣˊ 飄ㄆㄧㄠ 過ㄍㄨㄛˋ,

他ㄊㄚ 就ㄐㄧㄡˋ 唱ㄔㄤˋ 起ㄑㄧˇ 歌ㄍㄜ 來ㄌㄞˊ。

Tumbling left and right,
splashing up and down,
the frog tumbles and splashes in the well.

18

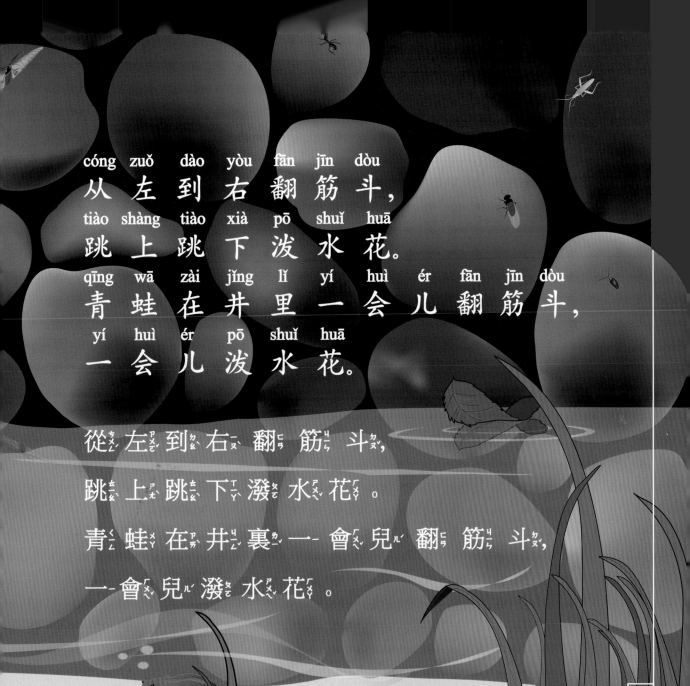

cóng zuǒ dào yòu fān jīn dòu
从 左 到 右 翻 筋 斗，
tiào shàng tiào xià pō shuǐ huā
跳 上 跳 下 泼 水 花。
qīng wā zài jǐng lǐ yí huì ér fān jīn dòu
青 蛙 在 井 里 一 会 儿 翻 筋 斗，
yí huì ér pō shuǐ huā
一 会 儿 泼 水 花。

從左到右翻筋斗，

跳上跳下潑水花。

青蛙在井裏一會兒翻筋斗，

一會兒潑水花。

19

A big sea turtle crawls to the well.

yì zhī dà hǎi guī pá dào jǐng biān
一 只 大 海 龟 爬 到 井 边。

一 隻 大 海 龜 爬 到 井 邊。

"Would you like to come into the water?" the frog asks.
"We can splash together. "

qīng wā wèn   nǐ yào bú yào jìn lái ya
青 蛙 问: "你 要 不 要 进 来 呀?
wǒ men kě yǐ yì qǐ wán pō shuǐ huā
我 们 可 以 一 起 玩 泼 水 花。"

青 蛙 问: 『你 要 不 要 進 來 呀?

我 們 可 以 一 起 玩 潑 水 花。』

The sea turtle shakes his head
and looks straight at the frog.
"Have you seen the ocean?" asks the sea turtle.
"No," the frog answers.

hǎi guī yáo yáo tóu
海 龟 摇 摇 头，

zhí zhí de kàn zhe qīng wā
直 直 地 看 着 青 蛙。

wèn qīng wā shuō nǐ kě céng jiàn guò hǎi
问 青 蛙 说："你 可 曾 见 过 海？"

qīng wā huí dá méi yǒu
青 蛙 回 答："没 有。"

海龜搖搖頭，

直直地看著青蛙。

問青蛙說：『你可曾見過海？』

青蛙回答：『沒有。』

"The ocean is big. The ocean is deep. The ocean is wide. The ocean is blue," the sea turtle continues.

hǎi guī jì xù shuō
海龟继续说：

hǎi shì dà de hǎi shì shēn de
"海是大的，海是深的，
hǎi shì kuān de hǎi shì lán de
海是宽的，海是蓝的。"

海龜繼續說：

『海是大的，海是深的，
海是寬的，海是藍的。』

"Life in the big, deep, wide
and blue ocean is wonderful!
There are many other creatures in the ocean."

shēng huó zài yòu dà yòu shēn yòu kuān
"生活在又大，又深，又宽，
yòu lán de hǎi lǐ shì zuì měi hǎo de le
又蓝的海里是最美好的了！
hěn duō qí tā shēng wù yě zhù zài hǎi lǐ
很多其他生物也住在海里。"

『生活在又大，又深，又宽，
又蓝的海裹是最美好的了！
很多其他生物也住在海裹。』

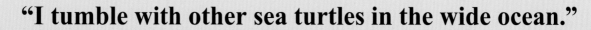

"I tumble with other sea turtles in the wide ocean."

26

wǒ gēn qí tā de hǎi guī
"我 跟 其 他 的 海 龟
kě yǐ yì qǐ zài dà hǎi lǐ tiào làng
可 以 一 起 在 大 海 里 跳 浪。"

『我 跟 其 他 的 海 龜
可 以 一 起 在 大 海 裏 跳 浪。』

After hearing the sea turtle's words,
the frog's eyes widen and his jaw drops.

The frog is startled and awakened.

tīng le hǎi guī shuō de huà
听 了 海 龟 说 的 话，

qīng wā zhēng dà yǎn jīng zhāng dà zuǐ bā
青 蛙 睁 大 眼 睛，张 大 嘴 巴，

fēi cháng de jīng yà bìng dùn shí xǐng le guò lái
非 常 的 惊 讶，并 顿 时 醒 了 过 来。

聽 了 海 龜 說 的 話，

青 蛙 睜 大 眼 睛，張 大 嘴 巴，

非 常 的 驚 訝，並 頓 時 醒 了 過 來。

29

The frog is embarrassed by thinking the well is the world.

He is wrong about being the greatest and the smartest.
He learns that there is a bigger world outside of the well.

青蛙对于过去以为这口井
就是全世界，感到很惭愧！
青蛙以为自己是最伟大，最聪明的。
青蛙学习到，井的外面，有更大的世界。

青蛙對於過去以為這口井
就是全世界，感到很慚愧！
青蛙以為自己是最偉大，最聰明的。
青蛙學習到，井的外面，有更大的世界。

"The frog in the well" is a Chinese idiom to describe a narrow-minded person.

If a person is like "the frog in the well," then he thinks he knows a lot.

If a person is like the turtle, then he knows there is an ocean of knowledge for him to learn.

井底之蛙是一句中国成语，
用来形容一个人的世界狭小。
如果一个人是井底之蛙，
他会自认为什么都知道了。
如果一个人像那只大海龟，
他会知道总是有更多事情
值得去学习。

井底之蛙是一句中國成語，
用來形容一個人的世界狹小。
如果一個人是井底之蛙，
他會自以為什麼都知道了。
如果一個人像那隻大海龜，
他會知道總是有更多事情
值得去學習。

About the Author

Irene Tsai, Ph.D. was born in Taiwan and grew up in Queens, New York. She believes books can change lives. Indeed, books have motivated, challenged, and reassured her throughout her life and into her career as an engineer. Growing up in Flushing, New York, Irene spent many hours reading books in Chinese and English in the Flushing Public Library and Chinese Culture Center. She credits her ability to communicate in both Chinese and English to her mother, who loved reading Chinese literature and watching traditional Chinese movies. Irene has published articles in the *World Book Encyclopedia* as well as scientific journals. You can find out more about Irene at http://www.cebilingualbooks.com.

About the Illustrator

Pattie Caprio has been a visual communicator for over 35 years. She received recognition for her artwork at the early age of seven. Pattie was inducted into the National Honor Society, Phi Theta Kappa, in 1996. In recognition of her outstanding contribution to the *Preservation and Appreciation of the Heritage of the Upper Delaware Valley*, she received an award for illustrating *Falling Feathers: The Pocono Indian Presence.* Her award-winning logos have also brought Pattie national attention. Pattie served as an art director for a Pocono magazine located in Pennsylvania for 13 years. She was an art director for an advertising agency in 1973 in Dalton, PA and became the art director for the Native American Pavilion Project (NAPP) for Native Americans in 1992. Her dedication to the work of the NAPP earned her the honor of an invitation to President Bill Clinto Inaugural Ball. Pattie owns and operates a professional graphic design firm, Caprio Graphic Design, since 1974. Please visit her website at http://www.logosanddesign.com.

English	Simplified Chinese	Pinyin	Traditional Chinese	Zhu Yin Fu Hao
Hop	跳	tiào	跳	ㄊㄧㄠˋ
Tiny	小	xiǎo	小	ㄒㄧㄠˇ
Hungry	肚子饿	dù zi è	肚子餓	ㄉㄨˋ ㄗˇ ㄜˋ
Beautiful	美丽	měi lì	美麗	ㄇㄟˇ ㄌㄧˋ
Ocean	海	hǎi	海	ㄏㄞˇ
Creatures	生物	shēng wù	生物	ㄕㄥ ㄨˋ
Right	右	yòu	右	ㄧㄡˋ
Left	左	zuǒ	左	ㄗㄨㄛˇ
Moon	月亮	yuè liàng	月亮	ㄩㄝˋ ㄌㄧㄤˋ
Frog	青蛙	qīng wā	青蛙	ㄑㄧㄥ ㄨㄚ
Eyes	眼睛	yǎn jīng	眼睛	ㄧㄢˇ ㄐㄧㄥ
Water	水	shuǐ	水	ㄕㄨㄟˇ
Little	小	xiǎo	小	ㄒㄧㄠˇ
A fly	苍蝇	cāng yíng	蒼蠅	ㄘㄤ ㄧㄥˊ
Long	长	cháng	長	ㄔㄤˊ
Tongue	舌头	shé tóu	舌頭	ㄕㄜˊ ㄊㄡˊ
Wide	宽	kuān	寬	ㄎㄨㄢ
Deep	深	shēn	深	ㄕㄣ
Head	头	tóu	頭	ㄊㄡˊ
World	世界	shì jiè	世界	ㄕˋ ㄐㄧㄝˋ
Sea Turtle	海龟	hǎi guī	海龜	ㄏㄞˇ ㄍㄨㄟ
Tumbling	翻筋斗	fān jīn dǒu	翻筋斗	ㄈㄢ ㄐㄧㄣ ㄉㄡˇ
Happy	快乐	kuài lè	快樂	ㄎㄨㄞˋ ㄌㄜˋ
Down	下	xià	下	ㄒㄧㄚˋ
Up	上	shàng	上	ㄕㄤˋ
Big	大	dà	大	ㄉㄚˋ
Bigger	更大	gèng dà	更大	ㄍㄥˋ ㄉㄚˋ

Word list is continued on page 36.

Word list is continued from page 35.

English	Simplified Chinese	Pinyin	Traditional Chinese	Zhu Yin Fu Hao
Blue	蓝	lán	藍	ㄌㄢˊ
Clouds	白云	bái yún	白雲	ㄅㄞˊ ㄩㄣˊ
A well	一口井	yì kǒu jǐng	一口井	ㄧˋ ㄎㄡˇ ㄐㄧㄥˇ
Idiom	成语	chéng yǔ	成語	ㄔㄥˊ ㄩˇ

WORD LIST FOR THE FROG IN THE WELL

"This is a beautiful children's story with entertaining and compelling illustrations, as well as a worthwhile story line. The English and Chinese translations provided on each page are sure to help young readers become masters of both languages."

-Cynthia Maro Saracco, Author and Public Speaker, CA

"Introducing a child to stories like *The Frog in the Well* opens a whole new world to the young mind. It is a wonderful idea, both through storytelling and the accompanying artwork. Well done!"

-Peggy Bancroft, Author and Editor, PA

"I have had an interest in China ever since a 4th-grade teacher opened my eyes to the country and its people, culture, language, and history. *The Frog in the Well* will create a spark for learning about China and the most spoken language in the world: Mandarin Chinese. Parents, teachers, and educational leaders should be encouraged to help children discover China, and *The Frog in the Well* is a great tool for doing so. Doing so will help prepare our children for the transformational world that they are entering and make America a magnet for Chinese investment in the future. Don't just sit there—hop on over and pick up a copy of *The Frog in the Well*."

-Tom Watkins, Michigan State Superintendent of Schools (2001–2005)
Honorary Professor, Mianyang University

The End

jié shù
结 束
結 ㄐㄧㄝˊ 束 ㄕㄨˋ